CONTENTS

CW01500149

1

3   **55**

A HOOK IN THE MILK SHED

A HOOK IN THE MILK SHED

ROBERT ETTY

To Tony,

Best wishes,

Rob Etty

8/1/14

GUITAR BAK

Shoestring Press

All rights reserved. No part of this work covered by the copyright hereon may be reproduced or used in any means – graphic, electronic, or mechanical, including copying, recording, taping, or information storage and retrieval systems – without written permission of the publisher.

Printed by imprintdigital
Upton Pyne, Exeter
www.imprintdigital.net

Typeset by narrator
www.narrator.me.uk
enquiries@narrator.me.uk

Published by Shoestring Press
19 Devonshire Avenue, Beeston, Nottingham, NG9 1BS
(0115) 925 1827
www.shoestringpress.co.uk

First published 2013
© Copyright: Robert Etty

The moral right of the author has been asserted.

ISBN 978 1 907356 86 5

ACKNOWLEDGEMENTS

Acknowledgements are due to the editors of the following publications, in which these poems (or earlier versions of them) first appeared:

14 Magazine
Assent
The Bow-Wow Shop (online)
The Dock (online)
Dream Catcher
English in Education
The Frogmore Papers
The Interpreter's House
Iota
London Grip (online)
Morphrog (online)
Obsessed with Pipework
Other Poetry
Poetry New Zealand
Prole
The Rialto
Seam
Smiths Knoll
Sunk Island Review (online)

1

ON A GREEN LANE IN THE AFTERNOON

The green lane alongside Pickering's Wood
in the patchy shadows of half-past four
with grass stalks wagging slightly and sissing
and Clump Hill Farm brown and grey on its rise
is a place not to let the past dog your heels
or be in two minds about being unsure
but to feel the air at your unbuttoned neck
and look at rose hips, and blue flies on leaves.

I was walking there and it was September.
Buzzards were circling ellipses of sky,
swallows swerved in and out of spaces,
slavering cows' dewlaps wobbled and swung,
and September was as it usually was.
Sunlight lit on the shape of a fox,
gingerish at the foot of the hedge
that was leading me round a bend in the lane.

The fox didn't see me or hear me or smell me,
but stared as I closed in on where it sat
across the field at something or anything.
Then it stood slowly, yawned, showed me its rump
and began to pick its steps through the grass.
The grass was warm, the puddles crazed,
sun and what breeze there was in our faces,
and neither of us saw reason to hurry,

but the hawthorn hedge suddenly rattled
and snapped, and a wood pigeon clattered
out of the foliage, shakily steadied
and launched overhead in a clapping arc.
As it flew across, the fox cowered and peered,
and its gaze fell from pigeon to me.
Then the nettles it slipped into closed behind
and gnats brought news of the following day.

A LINCOLNSHIRE WHIRLWIND, 1936

Most of them were there – Dad, Grandad, Grandmother,
the harvest workers – in the oak tree field,
but all with eyes down haymaking, and such
a baking sun, so no one saw it till
it struck. It whipped some drying heaps up in the air
and funnelled them across Bill Dashford's
milking shed and pasture to the lock
and dropped them there. Grandad hitched the rully
and they raked a full load up. Dad said
Grandad said the bloody next would take him, too.
It did, of course, and came back for the rest.

AS I WALKED OUT ETC.

It being the morning of Leap Year Day, out
I leapt with
spring in my step. Both the donkeys
up at the oil field nodded that everything
would be well,
and the water pipe-laying men looked joyful

in yellow on JCBs.
Chaffinches checked on the hawthorns' potential,
and redshanks sentinelling the marshes
took off in sequence and hooted
and whooped
to let me know I was almost there.

Since this is knowledge you're grateful for
on a day that quarters the time
you've lived
and also the time you haven't, I surprised
myself by offering thanks
(inasmuch

as a person can thank a redshank)
and strode along
past molehills and snowdrops,
16 again
with a silver plane roaring right overhead and nothing
to do but walk.

HEDGE TAKES DITCH,

Mr Sharnlow replied when I asked him
to clarify where I stood with regard to
dividing his field from my garden.
Since the first man, he said, (God knows when)
stood facing his own land and dug out the ditch
and planted sprigs in the spoil, it's been custom
and practice: a hedge takes a ditch, all the width of it.
So I own the banks, the nettles, roots and rat runs,
the sycamore wings that twirl onto the water
and swivel till currents whisk them off. And
the currents themselves, part rain from the road
and part local springs, touching and not
touching bed and banks, both held and always
releasing themselves, like anything unpossessed.

NIKOLAUS PEVSNER'S OTHER BOOK

Reused Roman stone in nave and chancel,
Pevsner writes, and much of south aisle rebuilt
1886. Chancel arches wide
and Early English. Fine sedilia.
Font (octagonal, ornate) shows flowers,
and angels underneath, two missing noses.
Outside restoration's overdone, he thinks,
as if atonement for the sins of sun and frost:

no fooling such a searching eye about
how much a block of stone can hide. Inside,
too, he traces lowered floors, works out
where doorways led and wonders whether
hollow-chamfered transverse arches were
the wisest choice. Clee, Claxby, Claxby
Pluckacre and Claypole, Claythorpe, Cleethorpes,
Legbourne, Legsby, Lincoln's long perambulations:

Lincolnshire's North Sea-aired naves, chancels, transepts,
pointed-trefoiled tomb-recesses, stiff-leaf knobs
and quadripartite vaults are noted down, with
halls and clock towers, schools and railway stations
part-way from antiquity to where we
are (or were when he stopped noting down).
It seems no stone or gold or wood's left out, but,
like the scallop worn from every chancel step,

the spaces everywhere define themselves:
the gap, for instance, in the holly hedge
along St Faith's south boundary, that Dick trimmed
as a short-cut from his bonfire patch to climb

the tower and wind the clock, and toll the bell
for funerals – the gap four muddy-trousered
bearers humped his coffin through that Friday
someone else was found to toll the bell;

the places under slabs the cars park on
that aconites turned yellow every spring,
and that damp cavern in the yews they sawed
the roof off so the lovers lost their nest,
and ghosts kids said were chained up there flew out.
Pevsner lists leaved capitals and two brass plates
from 1430-odd, but couldn't
have a clue that what was also worth a note

was who threw Psalters from the battlements
while Mrs Steed was hoovering the mats;
why John Ward Wood, whose tombstone's cock-eyed
in the sandy soil the rabbits dig and pile,
was laid one August day to rest right on
the far side by himself; the Manor window where
the lads took trembling turns to gape in
when Mad Mavis took her skirts off by the fire.

It's not to say he *should* have had: that would
be another book, dust covered, copyrighted,
with a glossary of terms to clarify
how each step forward paved a way, or
blocked it, for the next (though most things ended up
the best for someone – and the ones things
ended worse for learned to live with it), but
that's no gazetteer. Here's Clixby (part-restored).

THE THING ABOUT THE PEOPLE ACROSS THE ROAD

Thomas and Frances, Thomas and Gertrude,
Thomas and Annie, Francis and Freda
have nothing to say to each other or us.
Sidney and Alice (*Eternally Knit*) have lost
their tongues, too, like Mary Ann (5), Lucy
(11) and Ellen (16), in the nettles.

The Greenwoods lie under the sycamore tree
near the Sheardowns and Cornwells and Outwells
and three Albert Dashfords ivied together
with Lawrence the pilot, John Theobald M.A.,
Smith, Smith, Smith and Smith, Stokes of Stoke and
May Welfitt (*Died Sadly in Melton Mowbray*).

May Jesus Thy Bitter Pains Assuage
Dear Partner of My Pilgrimage
Charles wished for his Martha, who may have concurred
before angels carried her off to her rest.
Under Mavis's name, a snail underlines
Affliction sore She long time bore

and a scuffling rabbit turns its scut on
the green Black Death mound the mower missed,
over which in a moment the heavens
have opened, and a wren and a blackbird
give vent to emotion and flit
from a rail to wet moss on wet stone.

Not a peep from God's Acre, except for
the wren and tick-ticking drops
through low leaves now and then, but nothing
to waken the dead or the living, who
live very close and have planning permission
for windows overlooking the neighbours,

who never gossip or take exception,
but keep in a neighbourly way
their own counsel about what it is
they could tell (if they could)
of how far into evening this rain will drag on,
or the thing about the people across the road.

DOLPHIN WINDOW

Pete has just cornered his flyaway cockerel and launched it
back over the laurel hedge when Malcolm's Jack Russells appear
on the path and hustle each other among the gravestones
and yelp at the feeling of being let loose.

Malcolm unlatches the bottom gate and calls to Pete (as he rushes
to check that his cockerel's landed) that these blessed dogs
are the devil's spawn. The blessed heat's to blame, he mumbles,
pausing with me by the porch in a sun-trap under the single-light
window.

He gathers his breath and his thoughts and reminds me
how this narrow window with the stone dolphin that history
conjectures
was carved *in situ*, probably in eleven-something,
reflects all his memories of Auntie Pamela's final wish.

Auntie Pamela died in Miami, swimming among the dolphins
she'd trusted to spirit away her oesophageal cancer and wave her back
to Doctor Deeley's on Cooden Drive, Bexhill-on-Sea, where he'd
hide disbelief
behind steepled fingers and privately study her X-rays again;

but Malcolm's unsure: is it Glastonbury Abbey where dolphins
are carved in the heads of windows, like this one we're standing
under?
Perhaps it is, since Glastonbury Abbey was Auntie Pamela's
pilgrimage place, and he always connects it with dolphins and her.

This dolphin might be a tadpole, a mermaid, a newt, a swallow –
erosion has streamlined it into them all, but the curve of its back
and the ghost of a fin bring dolphins leaping through sea spray to
mind
as they race the bows of boats with excited cameramen on board.

Mortar on one side's browned by rust from where a downpipe's
screwed in,
but, arced in its lintel against ochre sandstone,
the dolphin's unblemished and washed salty white by the rain
and wind
there's no shelter from between here and the marsh and the sea.

A starling with grubs in its beak still chitters. Nettles bow into the sun.
Think of it, Malcolm's murmuring: a man like you and me
tapping and chiselling
up there on a wooden scaffold or ladder, with only one chance
to carve his dolphin without making any mistakes.

He carved in late spring, I think, for the light, with sun in the beeches,
starlings whistling and clicking close by, these gravestones with
willows and urns
unhewn in an outcrop near Halifax, and Henry and Martha
Foggett *(Dear Wife)*
unconceived by their ancestors twenty times over; and leaned back

and scanned his final touches at ten o'clock by a watch no one had
on a morning in May when a bantam cockerel was bidding for
freedom,
and dolphins swam with believers in bays the stonemason never saw.
Then he walked where Malcolm's dogs went chasing, down
where the cowslips are.

LIKE A STORY BY H. E. BATES

I was walking along a country road, but without
an old knapsack or broken heart, and with somewhere
in mind to go. I'm not on the run, or a winsome drifter
who'll happily give any job his best shot, and I'm closer
to ninety than twenty. Swallows were wheeling and
swerving, but not in such numbers, I noticed, this year.
The soupy brown canal rippled idly. My digital watch
read 14.02. For more than an hour the sun had blazed
down, but rain would soon teem from a purple sky.
A black Chevrolet 4x4 steered round me, churning up
gravel that chinked as it rolled.

On the opposite side, a young woman appeared,
pushing a silver buggy. Why was she in this place,
so far from town, passing only a tidy bungalow
or a farm with no one in sight? Perhaps if I'd heard
the 2.25 puffing into the station through the fields
to take her and baby out to the coast… But that
would have been the station I'd walked from, if there'd
been a station there. She agreed that the afternoon
was nice, and became a pale smudge behind me.

There wasn't a pub called The Lock Keeper's Arms
behind the spinney a mile ahead where I took the time
to sip a light ale, and a lean man named Archie kept
his own counsel and half an unwelcoming eye on me.
There wasn't a BP filling station, or someone kneeling
weeding a grave, or a cat that was too hot to move
from a wall. Elderflower scented the thick summer air,
but the tractor I'd seen juddering over the verge had
scythed down the hemlock and meadowsweet.

I wished I'd been driving a blue Foden lorry
so I could park by the transport cafe and make up for
working my dinner hour. The waitress (30-ish, wavy
dark hair and a smile she'd learned to be sparing with)
would touch my hand when she had no need as she
served me sausage and eggs. As I paid, she'd say
Pop in again and I would, in my car towards sunset
one Saturday, and that's how we'd begin.

But I was on foot, and those long marsh roads are
much too lonely for transport cafes. In other respects,
it was straight off the page.

THE DUCK POND AT ETTON

It was ten past three by my watch, dead on,
when the red roofs of Etton rose over treetops
blown back in the straight-across wind.
Brian pulled his glove off and hooked back his sleeve.
"It's just gone five to nine," he said.
"If I wind this watch, you know, it stops.
If I twist my wrist, it starts again,
but I didn't twist my wrist today."
We sat at the duck pond at twenty past
on a Jubilee bench with its legs bolted down.
A woman shopping called when she saw us,
"Don't look for ducks on that blinking duck pond!
Somebody's culled the blinking lot!"
At half-past, nearly, as long-tailed tits flitted
where unculled ducks should be waddling and paddling,
we synchronised our standing up
and set off for Scorborough side by side
and six hours and several minutes apart.

SET-ASIDE

has no meaning for badgers.
In undergrowth their paws have pressed flat
they leave dung-piles next to their runs.
A tractor's tyres have crushed the grass, too,
but the badgers follow their own runs and paths
down banks and between the shedding bushes.
They cut a corner across the wheat that's been planted
for reasons beyond a badger. Tonight
in a half-moon they'll trundle underneath the oaks
where tiny seedlings are threading through
and drag clumps of clawed-up grass to their setts.
A reed bunting flits through a reed bunting's air
across the set-aside.

A MYXY RABBIT AT SOUTH COCKERINGTON

Being a rabbit, it doesn't suppose
(that is, I suppose it doesn't suppose)
that the history of its terminal sickness
spans nineteenth century Uruguay,
Professor Armand-Delille of France
(whose underestimation of rabbits'
escapological potential
let loose epidemics right across Europe)
and 1953's goings-on
on an over-rabbited Sussex estate,
when someone wily enough to do it
imported a stash of infected French rabbits
and freed them down local burrows.
And, being a rabbit, it won't have been told
that Parliament failed to declare it illegal
to let the disease run asthmatically rampant
via gum-jabbing fleas and determined mosquitoes
through England's cornflowered meadows and lanes.
The wind flicks its unglistening fur into whorls.
Myxomata bulge on its head,
and its eyelids, bulbous and seamed with slime,
blink as if it can see.
Perhaps, with myxomatosis,
a rabbit smells its own death on its breath,
but this one shows no sense of resignation,
no urge to put its affairs into order
and muse on the transitoriness of things.
It sniffs and squints into the spring sun and wind
and stumbles off, seeing and hearing nothing,
down the middle of the single-track road.

A THAW ON THE ROAD TO LINCOLN

Some traffic overnight froze to a halt,
but early tyres have cut ruts through and, since crisp sun
broke out, the snow that's catching it's begun to melt.
We drive in steady convoy with lights on
and steer along dark grey grooves in the white.
On the verges, tussocks and green patches
spread, and branches sprinkle snow under the weight
of fluffed-fat wood pigeons. Rough crosshatches
of set-aside emerge around ploughed fields.
White zigzags slither down the village roofs
as violet thins to blue above the wolds.
At Lincoln, snow's receding into troughs
of slush beside the dual carriageway
and lingering in mounds by gates and walls.
At ten the road's no wetter than a showery day
and, even in the hollows, last night's snowfall's
drawing back and letting earth show through,
as if deciding slowly to unveil
not the expected, disregarded view
but something other than was there before snow fell.

DECEMBER 5TH, IN MILD WEATHER

A dog barks. A cockerel crows. The dog's barks
carry across acres of brown and green land.
Rooks chitter and click in the highest branches.
A heron glides levelly over the field
and croaks as it flies, twice long, once short.
A barn owl swings white on the axis of dusk.

THE GATES

The gate on the bridge across the canal that clangs
as it closes and brings the tired Labrador
loping and barking

The gate with the latch at the end of the path
with the stockproof fence all the way along
to keep the horses inside

Raymond's gate where he's tied wooden laths
so that Sheba doesn't scramble under
in the grooves his tyres have dug

Then the churchyard gate, thin, black wrought iron,
with decorative rolls on top of each post
and freckles of ginger rust

And the kissing gate (where no one kisses) that opens
onto the field with the earthworks and smoke
from Malcolm's blowing across

The gate with no slats at the opposite corner
that overgrown hawthorns hide
for half of the year

The tubular five-bar gate wired to a wooden one
so that it's wider and cuts off the entrance
to Malcolm's yard and barn

There isn't a gate to the grassy track beside the canal
where the herons stand
and kingfishers fish their territories

Then the gate by the stile and the farmyard
with calves breathing warm breath
into the heart of winter

Then the stile and the aluminium gate
where the digger grubbed up the thistles and nettles
and printed long parallels in the mud

The gate that's a simple hinged steel triangle
held at one end in an iron bracket
screwed to the trunk of a tree

And the gate no one closes day or night
because there are neither walls nor fences
around the rest of the garden

The gate to the churchyard that hands have rubbed smooth
where redshanks call out
that something might happen

The gate with a slab on a chain that restrains it
and makes it heavy and hard to open
and drags it to fasten afterwards

The padlocked gate to the breeze block shed
where the pigs are gated
inside pig pens

Then the gate to the field
where the red bull grazes under the alders
in September

The gate by the rabbit-guarded hedge
to the path
to a field of winter wheat

And down the slope from there,
the gate to
a gate and a gate

RED TOYOTA

Often it's parked here –
sunset, early morning – where
the track slopes down
and the ground's less overgrown.

Some magazines are in the boot
(the shelf's been taken out),
a bottle, blanket,
a man's jacket

and crushed sandwich packets.
He's not here, the jacket
owner. He'll be past the trees.
The things they'd sort through would be these

if, on the dashboard shelf, with
sunglasses, phone and a cloth
to wipe the windscreen, he'd laid letters
for a parent, wife, his daughters.

UNDER THE TREES BY THE CANAL

We'd seen each other approaching
from when he crossed the bridge
and the blackbirds had trilled a warning along the bank,

yet, on this expanding, contracting planet,
where all the knowledge we know about
is under all of our noses,

when I said *Hello*
as we passed near the lock where the moorhens nest
he couldn't think of an answer.

IN THESE LAST HOT DAYS

I've thrown a stick for a border collie
I ate mulberries from the palms of my hands
I made a phone call across the Equator
I've clipped the willow, the alder and three bays and barrowed away
the cuttings to burn
I've watched a green tractor discing the field and the scatter of
gulls behind
I stood underneath the Market Hall clock and heard it chiming ten
I woke in the dark and raised the blinds and lay and stared at Mars
I've chosen not to interfere
I bought a dozen free-range eggs
I've been watching roofers replacing slates
I've been troubled by some mistakes I made
I saw three loud crows chasing a buzzard
I posted a card for a baby boy
I tried to think back to find out what happened
I went out walking without a dog
I've fallen asleep when I shouldn't have
The chimney sweep came and I made coffee for him
I thought I'd reached a conclusion
I brought in the washing and ironed the shirts

2

A MAN WITH SIX BAGS ON THE ROAD
LOOKING BRIEFLY UNSURE OF WHERE HE IS

He's a man you'd expect to be wise
to this hedgeless road's illusion of bending
gently towards the coast, when really
it's only a practised feint on its southbound course
between fields where red tractors are ploughing in
stubble we've hardly had time to get used to yet.
Some of the roads play these tricks in the flatlands,
seeming hell-bent on what's up ahead
while keeping their tendencies under wraps
till we've followed too far to turn back.
Perhaps he's lost track of his sense of direction:
perhaps it's the road that's his destination
and not the undisclosed end of it –
he read Kerouac by the beam of a torch
and supertramps' autobiographies,
and walked out one midsummer morning
with just a jew's-harp and some lemon puff biscuits
to find a groovier life than the one
he'd had nothing to draw a comparison with.
Or is he more like the man at the flap
of the tent in the yellowing hawthorns
whose laundry and cover the breeze is blowing? –
whose unrepayable mortgage repayments
lay at the root of that midsummer lunchtime,
the van and the Westminster Chiming doorbell,
those men with diplomas in moving sofas
who blocked the pavement with sofas they'd moved
and an unpaid-for plasma TV.
When no driver knows what's round the corner,
it's tempting improvidence leering at someone

with wristfuls of bags to whom landmarks appear as
they do to us, but appear it a little later.
So the man says (in an indirect way)
when I park in a gateway and hold out some silver:
Don't give it me, sir is how he puts it,
taking a route to the west of my car.
Sand Skier, 12 to 1, Market Rasen –
and wasn't the rainbow a sight for sore eyes?
The double-decker to Bourne swishes past
on a timetable that it's learnt by rote,
and he calls *Bon voyage!* from among his bags
and *Be sure you know you've got there, when you have.*

LOST VILLAGERS

A digger's clanking on Middledykes Lane.
The garden centre's been given permission
to level the earthworks in Pettinger's field
where the stable is with its tiles falling in
and the bones of a Datsun he set on fire.

Twelve year-old Anthony (youngest of six
by more than ten years, the son Pettinger
used to kick seven bells out of when he had
nothing to do, and shut in the chicken house
overnight after Leeds United lost)
took us to look there one damp Easter Monday
and stood in the hollows and ran up the humps,
explaining how his teacher had told them
a village that once was here died away,
and how he thought sometimes he heard its children
calling his name out over the coos of doves.

I still see Anthony telling us this
three Easters before he overdosed
on the paracetamols stacked in the bread bin
for Pettinger's hangovers.

The digger's level with Anthony's jaw.
It's filling his mouth with earth.

THOUSANDFIRES HALL

Kreutzmann and Angela saved for three years
for the swampy plot on Fodder Dyke Lane
that nobody else would have for a song.
They scratched up a home in a caravan
and set about building Thousandfires Hall
to 1966 regulations
for contemporary dormer bungalows.
Kreutzmann's dad was a Prisoner of War
who'd never gone back to Gelsenkirchen
to hear the tales of its thousand fires
or to work as a joiner again. He joined up
the floorboards and hung the doors
and stood back and grunted he'd rot before they did.
When Thousandfires Hall was keeping the rain out,
Kreutzmann's dad planted trees by the fence
(some firs a neighbour's wife didn't want)
so Peter and Kitty could play behind them
out of the cutting wind.

Now Kreutzmann's dad's unmarked in the churchyard,
Peter's never settled to much, and Kitty can't believe
she's a grandmother pushing a pushchair in Sheffield.
When autumn's made its mind up it's here
the firs reappear on the long horizon,
a keeled-over clump that drapes its shadow
around the dormers of Thousandfires Hall
and breeds fungus under the fascias and soffits,
and Kreutzmann's verdammt if he knows the reason.

WHERE ANNABEL IS

Annabel in a patchy green sunset
and white schoolday blouse her mother would wash
came elatedly down the clovery path
through gnats in the churchyard next to the river
as if moments before she'd been lying
silent in a meeting place no one could see.
She jinked through the iron kissing-gate,
passed tractors and pigsties and click-heeled home
with her arms crossed around herself.
Her body's lying ten graves away now
from where she might have been lying then,
under the wind that flicks scarlet leaves
and carries the sugary stink of pigs,
and under a stone with her own pretty name
and the name of the man whose second thoughts
were the thoughts he finally acted on.
The word for the twentieth century sickness
that worried at her from cheekbone to sole
like a dog that wouldn't take Yes for an answer
is sans-serifed by a modern blade
among tendrilled copperplate flourishes
in a molehilly plot with twelve level miles
between it and the edge of the sea.
Death brings its wealth of experience
and its knack of keeping one step ahead
to any churchyard that smells of pigs
with a broken column and wound-down clock,
and to separate places a river connects
with deliveries of tetchy swans,
and where shadows of herons shade the tussocks
that yellow frogs are caught longlegging through.

Annabel's lying incomplete still
in the layer of silver clay fending off roots
of eleven yews fruiting in autumn pink:
she's shorthand chiselled in dazzling granite,
a *Think Of What Annabel Did* anecdote,
a white blouse puffed by an end of light breeze;
she's the part that remained of a leaving,
the someone among the someone elses
that what seldom happens happens to.

INDICATIVE

There has to be something she's fallen foul of,
to be sitting in front of a hayfield gate
in the showered-on grass at four on a Friday.
Her arms in her pastel green summer jacket
are hooked behind the bends of her knees,
and she's burying her face in the frame they make.
Most of the walkers who pass this gateway
are walking a dog that refuses to sit,
or they're age-deniers in polo shirts
and flexible shoes and surprise they didn't bargain for
that things finally come to this.

Whatever it is that's brought her to this
is tagging along in case she slips free.
She raises her head and the smile
her tears are trickling into may as well
be a felt-tipped notice saying *Everything's fine –*
I'm tired – please leave me.

A counsellor's pauses might coax out gradually
why she's in damp grass cuddling her knees.
Not having (or having) partner or children
could head her list of anxieties, with backlogs
and credit cards close behind. Perhaps
she's lost what she thought made her blood flow
and found it didn't at all.

This scent on the breeze is crew yard manure
that a farmer's left unspread for too long.
The other day it was chicken muck
and last week it was pig. Signs and signals
are everywhere for reading, downloading
and happening upon: maybe she's reached

the end of a novel, discovered two tickets
behind the toaster, or let a phone ring
and ring. There's always a message winging
its way in search of a hazarded guess.
Her bag's spilling into a clover patch
and the whole scene's composing an explanation.

PAVEMENT LEVEL

In Costa they're letting their lattes go cold
to gaze at the entertainment outside.
A woman has been unable to move
since she fell on her side near the kerb.
The tall man who's elbowed through onlookers
kneels by her and asks if this happens often.
She says (with tremendous presence of mind),
On balance, no, she prefers standing up.

He comforts her shoulder. Some watchers pretend
they're not watching at all. The ambulance
is taking its time. Her cheek's compressed
on a glove someone's tucked there and drizzle's
gluing her hair. Underneath her's her coat,
shoeprints and her own dimensions in slabs
laid on aggregate, concrete and sand.
Below this there's subsoil with earthworms in it,
and roots, rims of cooking pots, kneecaps
and jawbones, and deeper (sub-subsoil),
less soil and more rock. Siren sounds swell
and shop fronts the ambulance hasn't reached yet
are Mexican-waving in flashing blue.

The woman who couldn't move can't move still.
She's gaining a fresher perspective on legs,
but the leg-owners find horizontalness
unsettling on a pavement. So it's quite a relief
when the paramedics descend with a stretcher
and stretch her out, tilt her and rush her off
somewhere, and everyone's vertical again.

SAMANTHA CAN'T BELIEVE IT

Megan's saying she can't believe it
and Samantha can't believe it, either.
It's five to nine outside Thoresway High,
as if they've gone back to 11BF,
when nitpicking Mr 'Buncha' Flowers
used to tick them off for purposelessness
or strutting in smelling of Polo Mints
slightly less than of Benson & Hedges.
It must be eight years since they sat by the window
ignoring their English Resit lessons.
They'd done it before – well, it *was* a resit –
and found it more tedious second time round,
if that was believable. But believable
is what it was: it's this that isn't,
this parking pushchairs outside the railings,
with schoolkids in purple tops brushing past,
as if they're invisible, or old.
Sam and Megan have each had an Alfie,
and neither Alfie is very patient with Mum
while she chats to the other lady. He wriggles
and tugs and considers crying, but Megan
and Sam say *Just wait, Mummy's busy!*
exactly as their mums said to them,
which is something else they can't believe.
It's the day of English Paper 2 in the Sports Hall
behind Thoresway High. Year 11
are filing in, being asked for silence
and leaving their phones on the bench at the front.
Wasps that will drift in through open skylights
are on the flight path to the Sports Hall already.
This pale blue June morning, Bernard Flowers

is strolling somewhere between home and the shop,
between then and now, thinking and doing,
belief and disbelief, caring and not.
He'd agree (if they'd listen) with Megan and Sam
on their temporal imponderable,
but they're out of earshot anyway, and time,
like a bad cold, stays for the duration.
Meanwhile the Alfies outcry each other,
house martins are returning to houses,
and all the school bells in town have stopped ringing.
Megan and Sam separate with a hug
and promises to text. That's enough
for them to believe in for now.

KEITH

If they'd kept Keith at school till he'd learned to read,
he'd be there this morning, dragging his bookmark
down row after row of undisentangleable
shifting words and following his fleeing
attention across the flat fields to the wood
where his house was, his dad's dogs, his bike and
the knitting his mother taught him that winter
she couldn't put up with his mithering.

When they freed him, Ted Sant took him on
at his farm to muck out the milking sheds,
ditch, scythe, chop, hoe, but never found anything
Keith could do well – except bike to the bottom field
at three, honk a hoarse honk that the cows
understood and ride back with the herd,
swatting rumps with a switch snapped from somewhere
and nudging hooves off the mown verge with his wheel.

Between scything and chopping, with Ted gone
for dinner, he'd bike to the beck and slide
down the bank to watch sticklebacks jabbing
and swivelling in shallows, needles of light
that he used to take home in a pickle jar
of pondweedy water clotted with frogspawn
and smelling of April and wet trees and places
that if there were books about he'd read them.

KEN SLIPPING AWAY

His neighbour tells the woman in the bobbly coat
how odd the whole thing's been. Less so the death (although
the way he went's been Chinese-whispered up the road),
but more the email saying he wanted to be driven
to the crematorium in his brother's white Ford van,
and with his brother at the wheel, in overalls.
He needn't even move his stepladders and paint.
No prayers, no music, no pat words about the good he did –
just bunk his box onto the belt and roll it down.
Your loved one needs a better sending-off than that,
his neighbour says: a family likes a sandwich and a sing.
He left a grid reference for scattering his ashes,
so someone'll have the devil of a job –
it might be on a motorway, or over Cleethorpes pier.
Even a trivial death touches a nerve.
Two people a month in the USA
die when a vending machine falls on them.
Ken wouldn't ever have wanted the fuss.

RAYMOND'S MORNINGS

Often he doesn't bother with bed,
but sleeps in his chair until four or soon after.
He stands at the sink swigging sugared tea,
looking out of the window as dawn brightens
through the high sycamores next to the church
and the first blackbird calls from the roof of his barn.
If a rat trots across to pick bird-table scatterings,
he opens the window without a click,
pokes out the tip of his rifle
and shoots it between its nose and its ear.
One morning last week he watched robins square up.
He tells it as if it were all of life.

RAYMOND'S MOTHER'S ENGAGEMENT RING

Prising the nugget of mud off a tine
of the fork he was double-digging with
to set leeks in the plot that belonged to him now,
he didn't dream her ring might be in it,

a marriage and more since it slipped her knuckle
while (she said later) she'd been pulling peas
for the dinner she'd fallen behindhand preparing,
when they both had to hurry to catch a bus.

He broke up its cast on the clay it was made of,
scratched off caked soil with his nail and pushed
a stick through where she'd pushed her third finger,
tilting her head, perhaps, as they kissed.

Then he folded a plastic bag around it
and carried it in his pocket home to soak
in warm water and *Fairy Liquid*
and watch mud float off its setting and shank.

It hung on a hook with some twine and his keys
until summer passed, and with summer its shine,
and he slipped it into a box in a drawer
for somebody with their own story to find.

RAYMOND'S THUMB

They told him the blade edge had scraped the bone,
but Raymond's left thumb's healing nicely now.
He was chiselling a joint on a gate at the Shaws'
when Adele drove up with the dogs and the baby,
announcing she'd need to stay for a while –
there were complications, things were murky –
so would that be ok? Phil's digging footings
to lengthen his wall and thankful there's been no rain,
an absence that's divided opinions
about what kind of a summer it is.
We see Ken at sunset occasionally.
His sister's concerned that he sleeps in the day
and won't let her throw out those queer concoctions
that fill up his fridge, or his shoeboxes
with figures stencilled on.
He walked the canal path as far as the sea
and walked back and wrote poems about redemption
and women he's never known.
But, as Raymond's mother said when he rang her
from Accident & Emergency
(a woman no longer surprised by surprise),
somebody's always doing something.

THE AFTERNOON RAYMOND'S MOTHER DIED

The moment it happened, his black old cat woke
in the kitchen and stepped to the doorway
of where she was lying in white cotton sheets
she'd been too still for days to crease very much.

It started to wail from deep in its throat,
with its jaws half parted and whiskers splayed.
He opened a window and dropped it outside
and telephoned Alice from down the lane

to come and take things in hand. Then he put on
his jacket and walked to the gate at the top
of the track that led through the fields
to the sewage farm near the trees and ditches

where blackberries were that they'd picked together,
and milkers Keith would round up before long.
He poked along hedges where hips and haws
signalled that this was the end of a season

it seemed they'd rehearsed the end of each year
since she'd moved her bed down to the sitting room,
where the sunshine beamed in on a summer day,
and she read *Woman's Weekly* and slept.

Alice was finishing off at the house,
and the cat scraped its claws down the jamb when he came.
As he let it inside, it howled, sudden and loud,
as if no one had howled yet, and somebody should.

THE WINTER FEED

See what I did? Raymond's father asked him
as they drank tea and a wind swished round the yard.
I stuck. Like shit to a blanket, I stuck here.
When people used to tell me, You can leave,
you're not tied here because your father was,
I said, Do you think that's news to me?
That I think there's a law that says stay here
when I've a van topped up with juice outside?
It seems a simple choice for a man to make:
he's humping weight as though there's clay clagged
round his boots that slows him down and holds him –
so he swings his legs and kicks it off
and soars up with the crows.
But I knew that I couldn't cut off clean:
I knew I'd only be me somewhere else,
and harvest's no more harvest there than here.
He turned the cold tap on. They swilled their cups
and took their jackets off the hooks.
The winter feed wouldn't stack up by itself.

CLOSER TO MOVING ON

Rats had come up through the garage floor,
so we shifted the shelves and tumble drier
and bundled old mats to one side. He was less
jittery, broggling a hoe into cobwebby gaps
and tipping boxes over. Every scuff
might have been a rat making a break for it.
We'd only found droppings and sacks chewed for nests
when one shot from a roll of bubble wrap
on the ledge above the window. It slipped
like a dribble of oil to the ground and pelted
across to the double front doors that the workbench
was pushed up against. Where we couldn't see it,
it gnawed a hole through, the woody sound
almost echoing.
Then, in the quiet, we filled up the floor joints
with ready-mix, binned paint tins and jars,
swept round and hoovered, and knocked a cupboard
apart for burning.
Dusk came early and cold. He padlocked the doors.
The emptier now, the easier the next time.

THE JOURNEYS THERE

The man on the radio lamenting our forests
is saying a squirrel in Robin Hood's day
could have crossed from the Irish Sea to the Wash
without its feet ever touching the ground.
I'm crossing the Lincolnshire Wolds on four tyres
as a peachy dawn draws up its blinds
and pheasants in frost shine like Chinese teapots.
A contact lens has flipped out of your fingers
onto a carpet in the South West:
you kneel and find it and then lose your keys
when you ought to be hurrying down the towpath
in time for the 8-17 to London.
I catch the 7-56 from Newark,
watch trackside trees leave each other standing
and cross the point south of Grantham where
a squirrel's branch-to-branch route to the Wash
would have intersected mine.
For King's Cross a week and a half before Christmas
it isn't busy at twenty past nine
as I'm scrunching a ticket into a bin
and turning onto the Euston Road.
Now's when I think you'll be pulling in,
but you aren't (as you'll tell me, step by step,
later, accompanying squirrels crossing Hyde Park),
because of your lens and the keys you find
under the junk mail you've picked off the mat
addressed to the lady who works in the card shop
who used to live where you live.
When you phone me to say you're an hour
behind – when I'm into my stride on
the Euston Road in my lightest shoes

and a London with urgent affairs to attend to –
you throw me off course and I sit to reflect
on a seat placed for someone whose mind's not made up.
It seems best I meet you at Paddington
(three stations under- and over-ground)
and I'm there before the train you're on,
by the Best Sellers rack in WH Smith's,
keeping tabs on the board for arrivals
at platform 5.
I see you before you see me through the faces,
your eyes above queuing shoulders scanning
the concourse where we'll continue our journeys
on ground our feet haven't touched.

A TEXT MESSAGE SHE SENT IN A HURRY

Ten times since it arrived I've pressed the key:
I'll walk towards you and you walk towards me.

To make sure it's saved, I press the key:
I'll walk towards you and you walk towards me.

In case it might have deleted itself,
I press the inbox key:
I'll walk towards you
and you walk towards me.

NEARLY AT FULBROOK

Ducks churn and bicker over bits of bread
we've thrown, and hiss each other off. Swans
cruise around the squabble's cackling edge
disinterestedly, bills submerging once
or twice, wings cupped. A woman feeds fruit to
a little girl. More cars have gone without
our seeing, and the car park's open through
to dried-up fields. Up river, two white boats
blink in the green. We finish sandwiches,
zip up the bags. Some things creep up so soon.
The banks are shady round the picnic benches,
and the evening's all that's left of afternoon.

WHEN MY MOTHER LEANED OVER MY GRANDFATHER

(a stableman, farm hand and topiarist)
in the final hours of his final pneumonia
with another spoonful of lukewarm broth,
he eased her arm away and asked her,
Do you know where I am?
Of course, she said. You're here, with me.
No, love, he said, in what might have been the last
of his voice, I am between a sailor's home
and a sailor's rest.
Or did he say, she wanted to check with him
afterwards, because of the difference it made,
No, love, I am between
a sailor's rest and a sailor's home?
Definitely, it was one of these,
and she passed it to me for the list I'd be writing
of Problems for Coming Back To on Wet Afternoons.

THE DOG DAYS, THE DOG DAYS

Heber stepped out of the shade in his brown cap and waistcoat
prodding a stick at some bullocks that we couldn't see for the hedge
until two by three and four they stumbled over the crumbly mud,
and their hooves clocked slipperily on the grey tarmac.
"Coom on an' 'elp me leäd 'em yon, sither!" he called above them,
so we ran across and stretched our arms out and slapped the bullocks'
black and white haunches and hustled them up the dazzling
                                                    green lane,
while Heber strode achily up to the gate and bumped it open
over the grass, and the bullocks shunted each other
into the air-raid shelter field. Heber was anxious and red in the cheeks,
and the sweat smelt sharp in his unbuttoned shirt
as he fingered some sixpences into our hands.

And one afternoon we found big Bruce Cresswell (whose mum
drove a Mini and dad a Rover and lived in a two-chimneyed house
on the High Street) sprawling on the top of the shelter, smoking.
Blue flies were settling on the hot concrete and swivelling
and rubbing their legs. Bruce stubbed his cigarette out on a frog,
and it scorched with no sound, but I hear it now.

3

"A PLUME OF SMOKE SOARED UP SUDDENLY FROM HER FATHER'S CHIMNEY"

(Thomas Hardy, *Tess of the d'Urbervilles*)

Downward she trod, down the grassy valley,
and picked out through morning mist and the trees
the roof of her father and mother's house
where she knew she could enter without a knock
and kneel at the fire that the smoke came from.
Her mother was boiling the day's first kettle,
poking oak twigs underneath it for heat.
The click of the latch was Tess's click,
and she turned, crossed and hugged her,
smearing the drops on her cheeks and her hair.
Tess whispered into her mother's neck she was
pregnant, but there was no man to bring home.
In the moment before her mother rebuked her
for not, at the least, securing his promise,
the moment that each of them had to make right
or let drift with all the world's unrighted wrongs,
Tess glanced at the family things in their places,
taking the shapes they had always taken,
but none of them looked today as it used to.
The way of this would elude Tess still
as she milked, threshed or grubbed turnips, long
after her mother pronounced it God's pleasure,
and said she supposed they must get on and do.

THREE BOOKS ABOUT CATS

Brought up so well to respect my betters,
tall ladies with long teeth, my teacher,
the barber, the Rector with his surgical boot,
Miss Gaffney next door
who worked in the laundry
and every book that came into my hands,
I stooped to pick up three square, yellow hardbacks
of Would-You-Believe-It? yarns about cats
that I'd knocked with my jacket off the rack
alongside the queue in Waterstones.
The woman I almost bumped into behind me
(who wasn't irritated or impatient
and gave no hint of her feelings for cats)
stepped back and said with a terse kindliness
as I ran my fingers along the rack
to find the pile they'd fallen from,
For Christ's sake, just leave them.
Just leave them. Don't worry.

READING ANITA BROOKNER

The eyes of the girl in turquoise shoes
seem not to be moving across the page
that she hasn't turned all the time she's been nestling
into the leather chair next to Self-Help:
she may be mulling over the line
she was reading when concentration flagged,
reprocessing words without looking back;
or something else might have occurred to her,
such as whether it's wiser to wait and watch,
why we say what we didn't expect to say,
why the teenager fingering Fantasy
with *Necrophile* on his T-shirt in pink
wasn't sent upstairs by his mother to change
or else he could cook his own spinach dhal.
Perhaps I'm guessing she's thinking these things
because I'm thinking about them myself
in the aisle between Art and Painful Lives
with a paperback Anita Brookner
that I breathed in the smell of before I sat down
on the sofa that's altered my view.
A couple in reading glasses unfold
a red concertina with *Portugal* on it,
rotate it clockwise and pick out the place
where they camped in '08 that was very nice
but further inland might be nicer this year,
while the man at the table is picking up
books about aeroplanes from a small pile
and studying photographs on the jackets.
Buyers queue pensively at the tills,
skimming blurbs and first chapters or gazing ahead
with scents of espresso on their coats.

People I used to know or know now
float between lines by Anita Brookner
in daisy chains of ideas and pictures.
They recede when I concentrate on her words
to the margins and space that is always there
when we look up from reading now and then
to leave ourselves and our books behind
and live lives we live when we're not living this one.

THE SAMPLING OFFICIALS

Rembrandt's final big commission, that he
earned as much for as a baker in a year:
five experts, each black-hatted, round a table
corner-on, with one bare-headed servant
who's learnt servants shouldn't push themselves.
Two youngish men look out from where they're
making sure this sample cloth's the quality
demanded in a town like Amsterdam.
They're wearing longer collars than the rest,
and longer hair, as young men did. One's jaunty;
one (though you could argue this) more supercilious,
measuring Rembrandt up while Rembrandt measures him
with loaded paintbrush and an artist's
vanishing point of view on the world.
Depending on how much you think can be
drawn out of tone and line, you'd feel
inclined to say he has an inkling
that for Rembrandt it's a downhill slope from here:
seven years, and then a debtor's burial
in the Westerkirk, a dateless slab they'll lever up
less than a generation later
and sling all his bones it hardly matters where.
There'll be a plaque, of course, given time, that skirts
around the disinterment of the poor –
but how could they, back then, have known
that Rembrandt's weren't just any bones, and which were
Rembrandt's anyway? The plaque records that
Titus van Rijn (son, deceased) was buried
by this pillar, so the chances are
his father was, as well. That's near enough,
its copperplate makes plain to those who like
a meaning with its cards close to its chest.
An eighteenth century hand signed *Rembrandt*

1661 across the chimneypiece,
too late for Rembrandt or a sampling man
to point out it was 1662
when he stepped back and wiped his brushes clean.
Still, what's a year, when bones are lost, long collars
shorter, and the brown moustaches of
the sampling gentlemen who held such sway
in Amsterdam are not moustaches but
brown paint brushed on to last who knew how long.

MADAME CÉZANNE'S PRIORITY

With acknowledgements to Marcel Brion and Frank Elgar

His sketching on location done, he laid
a palette for a morning in his studio
on the detail of *Le Cabanon de Jourdan*,
but the fever he'd gone down with on the road
to Tholonet (that stormy day the driver
of the laundry waggon found him, drenched
and chilled right through, and carried him back home)
took hold and brought him out in shakes so fierce
he couldn't guide his brush. He stumbled
back to the rue Boulegon and sank across
his bed. At noon, his cook arrived and knew
(as women would) this was pneumonia.
She sent a letter telling his son Paul
to leave for Aix at once and, if he'd been
the one the postman gave the letter to,
he'd certainly have left without delay.
But, as it was, Hortense, his mother, put
the envelope inside a drawer until
she'd been to have a fitting for a dress.
The cook, who stayed beside Cézanne's bed
as he lay, remembered how his clouding eyes
fixed on the door to see it open and Paul
walk across and kneel to kiss his brow,
and how Hortense's face looked when
they finally rushed in.

GOOD NEIGHBOURS

Their curtains went one Thursday. Then his car.
So what we didn't want to think was happening
really was. The waves, the held hands, "we're
a loving couple", screened the shattering

of the singleness they'd been. We'd catch them shopping,
strolling with the kids – small things that quelled the doubt.
But, looking back and knowing, gaps were opening
up between their different ways of being right.

Two weeks now since we saw their kitchen light,
but that alarm (no burglary, as usual) howled
at 3 this morning like a mardy afterthought.
At 7 (and I shouldn't), I gawped round

their windows at togetherness's parting shapes:
a grinning fuzzy bug slung downstairs. Envelopes.

TUI SINGING

Where the track lost its way in waterlogged grass
we leaned above the electric fencing to peer
down the pumice pit's slopes and ledges
at summits of tree ferns dropping below us.
Umbrellas across our shoulders struggled
to sheer off the rain and pummelling gales
that had sluiced the gulley since twelve o'clock.
Of the five we'd plucked from a tub in the garage,
the one I held, if not the oldest, had rounded
on Bay of Plenty winds more often than the rest,
and its sodden blue nylon wrinkled back
up the curve of a spoke it had given the slip.
Although the gale swooped under all our umbrellas,
mine seemed the one it tormented most,
flipping it uncontrollably from a bluebell
into a drumming tulip that briefly
endured a private winter and then,
with a whipcrack, shook rain at the rain.

The storm had almost blown itself breathless
when night hung out a hammock of moon.
Now tui are gonging in drying branches
and melody tipples into the kitchen.

IN THE MACKENZIE COUNTRY

The powder ground from rock heaving on rock,
descending in glaciers from mountains and valleys,
suspended in water and shot through with sunlight
stains Lake Tekapo as turquoise
as people say who've seen for themselves,
and cirrus scrawls the blue above the Alps.
The Church of the Good Shepherd watches over
a schoolboy rugby team breaking its journey
on white stones the water's lapping grey.
Blue-sided mountains step down to grassland
where unrustled sheep pause from grazing to gaze,
and good shepherds trust in the law and their quad bikes.
Lake Tekapo shines turquoise every twinkling winter day
while we're believing, twelve thousand miles from here,
the place we live in shapes what we'll become.
The Southern Alps fringe Tekapo Canal above
and below its long turquoise rim,
a remarkableness that the salmon farm workers,
who face their reflections all the time,
seldom trouble to raise their eyes to.

A POSTCARD TO LOTTIE, FROM WOONSOCKET

The city of Woonsocket began in 1883 at the junction
of the Chicago, Milwaukee and Saint Paul railroads.
Three days after the sale of the first lot, the first church
services were held in a carpenter's shed...
(woonsocketsd.com)

The coming was hard – such a time on the ship –
but now I am settling in South Dakota
and think it the finest place to be.
I live in a wooden house, not like Grimsby,
that stands by itself, with a porch where I sit
after supper to see the wide sky.
When I tell you this you will catch your breath:
I have found the Saviour here.
Tell Dad for me, please. I would tell him myself,
but I've only this card and one sheet of paper,
and you will guess who I want that sheet for.
And ask Annie to pray, and ask anyone else –
I need all your prayers and of course I will write.
I start to feel happier, but not happy yet.
Last month in Woonsocket three hundred souls
were saved (counting roughly) at open-air
services on Sunday nights. Keep South Dakota
close to your heart – it's where the Black Hills are!
I picture you reading these words as I write.
How does Annie look now? Is she sweet, as she was?
My Best Love and Wishes, from brother Jack.

I shall buy a brown horse for my trips into Mitchell
and send you a present and photograph.

This, when I sailed to find money and ease.

FRANCIS BAZLINTON RECORDS HIS JOURNEY FROM LINCOLNSHIRE TO LONDON IN AUTUMN 1780

With acknowledgements to Colin and Gwen Baslington

After Rideing all night arrived and Brakefasted
Spent my morning in the market
the Butchers meat was very Low Beef 2/6
Rode behind John Coupland to Frieston Slept there

went to Frieston Church heard Henry Linton preach
don't much like his manner of Delivery
went to dine at Mr Shepherds found them all very well
Mr Thompson was not at home found them all well

Slept at Bennington had pleasant journey to Peterborough
but from thence to Boston was very disagreeable
as the weather was Rainey and bad
in my way met with a very Rainey Storm

Rode to Horncastle Fair
in my Road stop at Mr Ashes
and Brakefasted with Miss Holdham Dined at Horncastle
Drank tea at old Mr Southwells

Went this morning to Boston market
Dine at the Red Lion staid all day there
sent a letter with a Goose to My Dear Wife
as a present from Mr T

Tuesday was bad Day and on Thurs
there was the greatest storm of Rain and wind
When I was at Fishtoft on Thursday
got promise of Mr Newtons sheep to sell

Brakefasted at Mr Couplands then returned to Mr Thompsons
In the afternoon Rote to my Dear Wife
as Mr and Mrs Thompson went to Mr Hutchinson Burial
Drank tea at Mr Walgraves slept at Mr Thompsons

in my Road to Tetford called on Mr Parkinson
had the pleasure of seeing his Lestershire Tups
think one is as compleat a Sheep as ever I saw in my life
and the other one as plain

After Brakefast went with Mrs Thompson
to Mr Evison to Mr Thompson wedding at Frieston
a very Dull Day for the Bride
there was only Miss Blith and Mrs Gothin there

Slept there and this morning Rode to Boston
dined at Mr Hubberts then returned
Slept at Mr Shepherds in the old Bed
where first I enjoyed my Dear Wife

Brakefasted at Mr Tophams then rode to Grantham
to Dine with my old friend John Rouse
then rode to Nottingham
where I arrived about 7 o'clock

I think Nottingham very ill built Town scarcely a good street in it
the market seems to be plentyfully suplied with Fresh Meat
but to Fish & Fowl and Garden Stuff
seems to be very dear indeed

Left Nottingham this morning
Dined at Lecester then came Bricxworth
a Traveller went with me on to Dunstable then to St Albans
I drank too much last night arrived in London about one o'clock

Brakefasted this morning at home
along with my Dear Wife and Sister who I found very well
and with Mr Waltham who returned home on Tuesday night
walked into the Borough and to Islington

Was all day picking Cranberries for Mr Waltham
to whom I sold 8 pecks and 3 quarts
in the afternoon went along with Sister Nancy
to her place at Mr Willson No. 252 in the Borough

Had 11 sheep of Sami Williamsons which took me all the day
as the middling sort was scarsen
To be got shut of Mrs Bazlinton & Sister
went to see the Lottery Drawn this day

HISTORY

Elizabeth Vance (who had sold her soul)
hanged herself from a hook in the milk shed.
Edwin Cocker, a cannibal, whose father received
twenty lashes for poaching and blasphemy,
ate horse flesh raw and never felt well in himself again,
but had three or four bastard sons by Joan Arnold
and died at forty of poisoning.
They found Peter Daft frozen stiff on the green.
He'd been drinking all night at Jeffrey Turbey's.
Dick Aldwood inherited Aldwood Farm from his father,
Dick Aldwood, and passed it on to his son,
Dick Aldwood, who passed it on to William (his son)
and his young wife, Suzanna, or Sukey.
William went out with his horses and waggon
to bring back coal on an icy night and developed
pneumonia that threatened his life, but survived and fathered
beautiful twins christened Sarah and Catherine-Anne.
William was crushed by a runaway waggon
and left his daughters with no memories of him.
Frances Parkin (Ned Parkin's widow) drank for two days
to stave off the cold and suffocated with the strong liquors.
Stephen Fox lost his first wife in childbirth
along with the tenth child she'd given birth to,
so he married again at sixty-six, had four other children
and took to his bed with a wandering mind.
James Heward, the vicar for twenty-nine years,
kept registers in a tidy hand,
but never seemed happy with punctuation.
Richard Aldwood, who's seventeen,
curled the Volkswagen that was his pride and joy
round a telegraph pole in the rain at night,

three weeks after passing his driving test.
Sally (the girl in the passenger seat) was whiplashed
and badly shaken up.
Richard's in hospital in town and the village is hoping
he's pulling through. His dad says he's better every day,
but he's not sure they're out of the wood.

4

CARE-TAKERS

Alistair said "Take care", so I took it,
in much the same way that I take a flier
for *Pizza For 2* if the hander-out
looks chilled to the bone and is clutching
a blue fistful more. I've never called in
to sample a pizza and didn't expect
the care to resurface, but here it is
at my elbow now, adding its weight
to assorted cares I stockpile about
my person. I'd gladly give it the push,
short shrift, a hard time, the elbow,
but *carefree*'s easier to say than be.
I understand Alistair more fully now.
Next time I see him I'll say "Take care"
and hope he's better at handling it.

PRECAUTIONARY

Don't find yourself without a piece of string,
a penknife and a pencil.
Carry some money, but only enough
for a chocolate bar, or a ride on the Tube,
or a taxi home if it's late.
Memorise two (at least) special phone numbers.
Watch for deceivers, hypocrites, cynics
and anyone who wants anything,
and recognise the signs.
Remember it's true that "Every hero
becomes a bore at last."
If someone presses you, don't be afraid
to say you're afraid you don't know.

Aunts and uncles advised me to tuck
these wise words up my sleeve for difficult times.
Money has been more helpful, in general,
than never being without some string –
except for the suitcase occasion in Paris
when string would have been precisely the thing.
I two-face up to duplicity now.
I became my own hero and bored myself.
There's no knowing how much I don't know,
but I think advice likes to bide its time
and keep its own counsel, trusting that hindsight
will have the last word. And there's string
in the cupboard under the stairs.

THE NAVY MAN

A tortoiseshell cat trickled down a wall
and landed as if its bones were melting.
These were the terms I thought of it in
as I walked home the long way thinking of terms
for what many people have witnessed before
and some have described in pieces of writing
largely about more remarkable happenings,
employing a cat incidentally in recreating
a setting somewhere. That man who talks
about the weather was wondering, as he often does,
whether we'd beat the rain or it would beat us.
Last Sunday he spoke of his years in the Navy,
but, finding no common waters there,
we turned to comparing the forecasts again,
concluding that both of us ought to get back
before it rained or the sun came out.
It's helpful that everyone knows so much –
it helps when you're writing about what you know
or you're stumped for something to say.
But you never expect to find on your doorstep
an utterly unexpected thing,
like a baby in a superstore bag
who's destined to alter the course of rock music
as much as Buddy Holly did – or two severed
body parts, leading the police to search
every nook for the rest of someone.
Or, staring at the half of a Mazda
that hasn't just entered your sitting room,
a driver who misread the black ice as shadows.
Because I tend to write what I know
(using the method the manuals advise),

I wasn't expecting this poem might
concern itself with the unexpected.
It's taking me quite by surprise.
I'll leave it now to go outside
and look for the Navy man. He'll soon be passing
expecting rain, and rain's what I think I'll write about.

FOUR MICE

Totemic in their narrow bottle
on the clear glass bottle bank:
four piebald mice, feet splaying like pink stars,
incisors bared for gnawing,
each on hind legs on a granny knot of tails
to nose the water level for last breaths.
Eight eyes stare sightlessly four ways across
the car park with its mounds of gravelly snow,
and anyone who's been snowed in for days
and carries clanking empties from a car boot
faces four drowned mice that look at first glance
like four living ones in a teambuilding game
where they'd all spill over the bottle top
to breed in comfort in cake shops and sock drawers.

ALSO IN

Three slow lanes of us ease off our clutches
to shunt where the car ahead shunted from,
swing gearsticks back into neutral
and chew, scratch, drum, stare, stop staring,
exercise patience and twiddle with dials.
Wish the wife was as dirty as this
is fingered in dust on a pick-up truck's flap,
as if, if she read it, she'd mend her ways.
And *ALSO IN WHITE* on the uncleaned white van
with the revving driver whose schedule's tight.
The days straightface us with such travelled lines –
and condom dispensers scrawled *Buy Me and
Stop One* or *This chewing gum tastes awful*,
an *i* blacked in when a house is *TO LET*
and the hotel room Bible signed *Best wishes, God*.
In the hand of the comic who missed the joke,
ALSO IN BROWN pulls up alongside.

PAUSING FOR SHEEP

It's the Shortest Day, and minus 3.
On the M40, approaching Bicester, the traffic
suddenly starts to slow and drivers who've driven
at sensible intervals find themselves tailgating,
brake and stop.
The woman on BBC Oxford tells us queues have formed
in the eastbound lanes between Junctions 9 and 10.
At Junction 9, a livestock truck's been rammed by a van,
and some sheep have fallen out of the back – well, one sheep
fell at first (now she's smiling) and all the rest followed it.

Another livestock truck's on its way,
and rounders-up will round up the flock (twenty-odd,
so the story goes, on the hard shoulder, jostling west
in a contraflow) and shepherd them into it.
We're such a spectacle, evidently, that two buzzards,
two kites and a helicopter with a white flashing light
circle or soar right over us (and, in the case of the pilot,
no doubt, observe that it's not every Shortest Day
you see sheep halting motorway traffic like this,
but even sheep reach the ends of their tethers.)

Apart from stretching legs and backs, or yawning,
twisting flasks, switching and flicking, lowering windows
to prove it's quite chilly and raising them again,
it's a tricky time for us all to fill.
A driver ahead has jumped from his cab to enjoy the delight
of a lunchtime stroll in an accident black spot made safe for a while
by sheep showing dirty pairs of heels. Others are peering
between the queues for puffs from exhausts or first-gear scurries,
but, as far as the bridge that's become the horizon,
vehicles line up like a domino push.

BBC Oxford tells Oxfordshire the M40 queues are lengthening,
the replacement livestock truck's at the scene,
but the runaway sheep are still running away,
and it's seventeen minutes past three on the Shortest Day.
It plays *Let It Snow* to pass the time and says Oxford's dark now,
and it's very cold, and it's Christmas in only three days and nine hours.
It's probably less cold in Oxford than here, where tail-lights glow red
like the fairy lights in a garden down all of our streets.
The helicopter clatters across us, climbs to the fuzzy yellow horizon
and out of the windscreen's top corner.

At three forty-seven, the valley invisibly bristling with frost
is a silver-blue ghost of itself. Our outlook's restricted to
an arc of dashboard, steam on the windscreen,
strings of red lights that drivers each side
have their own angles on, and what a nuisance it is.
M40 drivers, it's over, you're moving! says BBC Oxford
out of the blue. *Little Bo Peep's caught all her sheep!*
Engines explode, headlights beam out,
and rope on the back of the lorry from Stafford shudders
as the handbrake lets go.

There's no trace of found-again sheep in a truck,
but Junction 9's reopened for joining.
Heaters are thawing our thinking out,
and mirrors offer their quiet reflections on hills
sheep have grazed for donkey's years:
the chance that's there always is seldom seen coming,
the spanner, the spoke, the certainty nobody's sure about,
how lorries won't pass through needles' eyes,
and a sheep running free makes the heart soar and sing,
so it's something to keep a lookout for.

THE ESCUTCHEON, or A DREAM ABOUT TWO JOINERS

The shorter of the joiners says they've come
to mend the cabinet. I'm not sure that
I own a cabinet and don't remember phoning,
but I ask them in and show them round the house.
We find a cabinet upstairs along the landing
in a bedroom with net curtains blowing out.
I say, *I think I'm dreaming this. This bedroom*
isn't in my house. I hoover every room
on Thursdays and I've never hoovered here.
The taller joiner rubs his nose and shakes his head.
Well, I'm not being dreamt, make no mistake, he says.
I'm only ever dreamt in my own dreams.
I dream fast-action, cars and women dreams, in colour,
in big cities and on motorways. But still,
this cabinet you think you didn't phone about...
He opens doors and drawers and feels inside.
The hinges are performing well, he says.
The glass doors seem transparent and the drawers
have space in them for you to fill with things.
It's this escutcheon that's the root of it.
It doesn't cut the mustard, in my view.
He taps his pencil end against his teeth.
To get a brass escutcheon matching this
we'd need to order it from 1910.
He smooths his hair back in the manner
of a man who'd put his shirt on what he's saying,
and we kneel in line like wise men with no gifts
and ponder the escutcheon at the root of it.
Red tulips with blue stems and leaves are intertwining

on the carpet in the bedroom, on the landing,
and (though I can't see from where I'm kneeling) down the stairs
and through the hall onto the pavement of the street
in Doncaster that features in my favourite dreams,
but this dream's in a semi on George Cunliffe Avenue.
Ah! Yes! There's half a chance... , the shorter joiner hisses,
and his fingers spin a brace and bit
as if we've only seconds left before six guards burst in,
provided that the dream's not ending
and that this won't be the last line of the poem

THE MINUTE

In the dark of statistical evidence
that possessions and leisure bring misery
in equal measure to happiness,
that Christmas breeds suicide, greed and sleep
(and, for some insomniacs, divorce),
and that wrongdoers practise eluding comeuppance
and come up and wrongdo all over again,
I've been thinking about my halcyon days.
I've been thinking that if I'd known they were
I'd have paid attention, kept a journal
and countered what common sense was teaching
with *This is my never-returning fortnight,*
blue skies are bluer and brooks are more babbling,
the swallows have stayed and I'm not the same.
But a present like this one disturbs the past
and disturbance unsettles everyone.
People are wishing the weather would change,
so they could wish it would change again.
They're reading new novels by famous comedians,
stocking their cupboards with echinacea
and pricking their ears at expert advice
about listening to experts in troubled times.
Scientists are on the point of announcing
that certain types of cancers appear
to appear more often in taller people, but
that's not to say breathe again if you're short.
Icecaps are basking in global warmth,
cliffs are flaky, seasons unseasonable
and rats are feathering their nests.
These are the days that will cause someone
sometime to put aside whatever they're holding

and sigh for a reason they won't disclose,
What days! Ah, what days! What days they were!
Though it passes too swiftly to live for it in,
the minute's all there is to live for.
Days are tripping over themselves
to go where days go to (or where they come from),
and the past's nostalgic about how it was.

OUGHT TO HAVE

and (wiser, sometimes) ought not.
Ought was a word in the ear, a better
foot forward. It brought and despatched,
taught, tested, sum-totalled, exposed
at least forty levels of failure. It
caught you once and still catches you.
It's an afterthought and an aftermath, the
passport to where someone went without you.
Watch it contorting your going-out face as you
check your hair in the hall. Shortly your tongue's
tied, your guard's down, you're fraught
and resorting to mindful deep breaths. So
have you sold and bought to advantage? What did
your daughters not mention they knew?
Was drowning the kittens slaughter
passed off as mortality's guiding hand?
Ought was what somebody wanted for you
and oughtn't the other option. You've left undone
things you oughtn't to leave, and not
left some things you ought.
With support often less than it's held up to be
and forethought lagging behind,
you're out of sorts in a couple of ways you've
sought simple remedies for. Change alters cases.
You ought to decide. Look both
ways. Sleep on it. Trust water.

NOW THEN

A phrase commonly used in northern England... for greeting, although it is unknown as to why the terms "now" (meaning this instant) and "then" (meaning in the past) were put together to form another way of simply saying "hello".

(urbandictionary.com)

Down our little road, we slurred it to *Narn*
and used it daily, preceding *Dobbo*
or *Jonesey* or *Y'off out? I'll come round,*
which made us less likely than ever
to question how two adverbs juxtaposed
and out of context had come to mean *Hello.*
Now might make sense, in acknowledging that,
although we were itching to start on our futures,
the present was current and we were in it,
it was in us, and what could be more momentous
than that? So *then* made sense, too, as *now's*
destiny, its preconception and afterlife,
its fund of memories for fondly perusing
when being alive ceased to be worth living for.
And *then* was only a classroom behind,
as we squabbled now and threw things and loafed
and blotted the best copybooks in the school,
like our grandparents, who never dreamed
(yet never stopped dreaming) that it would be
our dads and mums they'd give birth to on hard beds
in hardship and swaddle in pillowslips
till neighbours clumped up the stairs bearing help.
Then was forever compounding itself,
inexhaustibly picking up our littered
ever-presents, banking experiences

that ought to have taught us that when they're completed
(if not finished with), the system assembles more
round the corner, like Mart with his airgun
or Fitz with ideas and *Now then*
the next words he'll say.

FORMER THINGS AND THINGS OF OLD

In the context of telecommunications,
an expert quotes from the Book of Isaiah
Chapter 43, Verses 18 and 19,
where Isaiah makes no bones about how we're
not to remember the former things,
neither consider the things of old.
It must be Isaiah's turn of phrase
that takes me straight back to the Evensongs
that mystified me when I was eight, sitting
next to my mother, third pew from the font,
and to women smelling of talcum powder
kneeling on hassocks in stiffness and silence
and suddenly becoming normal again.
Surely, all former things being equal,
suede-shoed Mr Cramp must have read
from Isaiah in all the lessons that rang
from behind the brass eagle lectern he'd crept towards
in much the same way as he crept up on
scrumping boys in his orchard. Mr Cramp
with suede shoes and a crackdown on scrumping
leaned slightly away in their personal pew
from Mrs Cramp, who had eyes like a stoat
and veiny legs and rose to be second-choice organist.
I wondered later was she as skilled as Alan Price
of The Animals, whose playing in 'The House
of the Rising Sun' was why my friend Graham
tried his hand on his Uncle Larry's piano.
Two policemen asked Graham and me serious questions
when Ernie from Lilac Lane vanished one Sunday
and (as it emerged) thumbed a lift with a vicar
who promised in good faith he'd take him

to Glasgow, but thought better of it in Brigg.
It turned Ernie into an atheist
(but I'd forgotten about him until now)
and might have been a lingering reason
he took himself off to teach English in Tokyo
and finally settled near Eastbourne. Ernie lived
opposite Snapdragons (where no one seemed
to live at all, but where snapdragons bloomed
as if someone did), which was on our route
through First Cow Field to the woods and the airfield
and out to the becks where, if we'd kept our interest up,
we'd have caught newts by the jarful. So they're best
unconsidered, these former things, such as how
Mrs Gaines gained three husbands quickly
and calamitously lost all three,
the father of five who hadn't invited the police
to his bomb site tryst that night, and Notright
Sharpe, who knew all about Sputniks and liked to lock
his dad outside and watch him sink into tears.
Let's not remember the things of old:
let's ignore how one old thing leads to
more that we'd thought we might overlook
because looking over was easier than at.
As well as exactly whose hair he was wearing
and whether the word he kept muttering was *fulcrum*,
there was something about Physics master Isaiah
(so named because one Isaiah than the other)
that I can't seem to put my finger on, but Isaiah
the Prophet warns not to disturb, and he wrote
the textbook, when all's said and done. They slipped
Prophet Isaiah inside a tree trunk
and sawed the trunk and Isaiah in two,
which possibly meant that his lifestyle tip

put at least one sawyer's mind at rest.
His tip might do the same for me, but for experiencing
former things and not really wanting not to.
Graham's front room smelt of bristly brown dog
and warm brown gramophone. His mum
used to bring in Battenberg cake, saying
keep the crumbs off the cushions, they're hoovered.
On the other side of the cul-de-sac
Clarky Clark once tipped scalding water down
his front when his mum went to answer the door.
Clarky was too nice to bear a grudge, but
he bore the scar and used to show us it
when we changed for PE. Former things
reappear in the mirror, resound in a voice
and never play themselves out in music.
I've checked, and Isaiah doesn't foresee
'The House of the Rising Sun', but all the same
he seems to suggest switching off
when they play it on Radio 2
if we think we might feel those pangs again.
And instead of remembering former things
(which won't make a way in the wilderness),
we should do a new thing and watch it spring up,
such as taking our cue from Mrs Gaines,
when she threw herself into living in sin,
convinced in her blood the day was at hand
when no one would trouble to bat an eyelid.

KNOW THYSELF AND OTHER PEOPLE

Mr Churchman worked in men's outfitting,
wore arm garters, expectorated in the bathroom
and was always first to a knock at the door.
There was a reason I didn't know
why I wasn't allowed to ride in his Wolseley
however nicely he asked me to. Aunt Elma
(not really, as someone said later) would
suddenly need something desperately and send me
off to Auntie Pamela's (not really, either)
at Klips 'n' Kurls on the road to the park
via the redbrick back alleys of Doncaster
that the sun only found a way to shine down
at certain times in an August day.
Uncle Willie, Aunt Elma's brother, was suffering
from Luftwaffe dreams and lung cancer,
which he joked about, but no one joined in
and Mr Churchman dabbed egg off his lips
and took himself off to expectorate.
Auntie Pamela and Uncle Derek lived noisily
near the V-Bomber base and turned up
the sound on their colour TV while
Vulcans were thundering above the estate
and both the china cabinets chattered.
We went to stay only when harvest was in
and Dad wasn't working as much. Uncle Willie
waved over the rail at the station stairs
as if we'd come from further than Grimsby.
In a voice like straw in a paper bag,
he said Elma was cooking a beautiful pie,
but ran out of breath before praising the pudding.
With Pat from next door we all sang 'The Ash Grove'

round the piano one Sunday, but shortly afterwards
Pat married Pete, who wasn't the singing kind.
Then the Wolseley was winched from under a bridge
with its steering column in Mr Churchman.
Uncle Willie died on the ward and Elma
fell down the coal cellar steps.
A thoughtful PS on my Christmas card
asked Derek and Pamela *How are you?*,
but what it really meant was *Who?* I didn't
receive a response to either – only news
they'd be moving to somewhere quieter,
omitting to tell me where. So away they all slipped,
leaving photos instead of answers to questions
the opportunity's gone to ask,
such as *Were they all lies about Uncle Willie?*,
Was Elma stone-blind, and what part did she play
in the consequences?, *Did Mr Churchman*
mean to do that? and about how some things can
change us into who we have always been.

IN PERPETUITY c1958

Not everything carries on for long.
Bad haircuts, bad colds and bad luck have their day,
but all of them face the fact that it's over
and leave us to cope with the aftermath.
When continuance drags on and on,
it's only a matter of sitting it out.

One Evensong when my trousers were short
I heard how Jesus told the Disciples (according
to Matthew, who wrote it down), *Lo, I am with you
always*. No one batted an elderly eyelid
along the brown pew my legs had stuck to.
Matthew had sounded convinced enough,
true lovers lived happily ever after,
and my mother thumbed me a Trebor mint.
Even unto the end of the world read the Rector,
a man able also to read children's minds.

Assured of these and other fragments,
I grew to witness longevities,
such as Mr McQuirk's unbroken attendance
at double Maths after Art on Fridays.
Double Maths seemed to exist beyond time
and Mr McQuirk was outwitting death,
but the dust motes in shifting shafts of sunlight
that halo all schoolkids when they're not looking
were not going to hang around.
Then the Rector drove off to a higher church,
a house fire outwitted Mr McQuirk,
and miscellaneous conclusions were come to,
not all of which were very conclusive.

Ending per se's never ended at all
and often The End begins something else.
There's a crucifix opposite Barclays in case
that's how believing works, and perfumes, rings
and aeons called *eternity*. Mr McQuirk
didn't cross my mind after Mr McConaghy-Dodd
took over, although it's clear he'd intended to.
I've been thinking I'll buy some longer grey shorts
and trot along to Evensong, but a good science book
might be more efficacious.

We've put the clocks neatly back where they came from,
and yellow leaves and the geese have landed.
Cycles like these, taking turns to turn-take,
create their own everlastingness. And
we've always had the between-times to live in.
Chances are we're between times now.

SCREENSAVER

When time travel's helping us make use of time,
I think I'll slip back with a digital camera
and take one shot for my screensaver
of the damson tree that half-shaded me
from the heat of a mid-afternoon in August,
with sheets on the line and the tin shed behind,
and the long olive grass that our small black cat
came threading her way through into the sunshine.

When I asked to photograph Uncle Tom
in his faded cotton drill Post Office jacket
pausing from watering his rows of onions
one day when it hadn't rained for weeks, he said,
'What better off shall you be when you've got it?'
Then Tom (who spent rarely, drank little, ate less
and never spoke ten words where two would do)
stopped still and held the stare of the lens.